Blown away

For Ally

First published in hardback in Great Britain by HarperCollins Children's Books in 2014
First published in paperback in 2015

10 9 8 7 6 5 4 3 2 1

ISBN: 978-0-00-759382-8

HarperCollins Children's Books is a division of HarperCollins Publishers Ltd.

Text and illustrations copyright © Rob Biddulph 2014

Visit our website at www.harpercollins.co.uk

Printed and bound in China

BLOWN away

Written and illustrated by

Rob Biddulph

HarperCollins *Children's Books*

A windy day.
A brand new kite.
For Penguin Blue
a maiden flight.

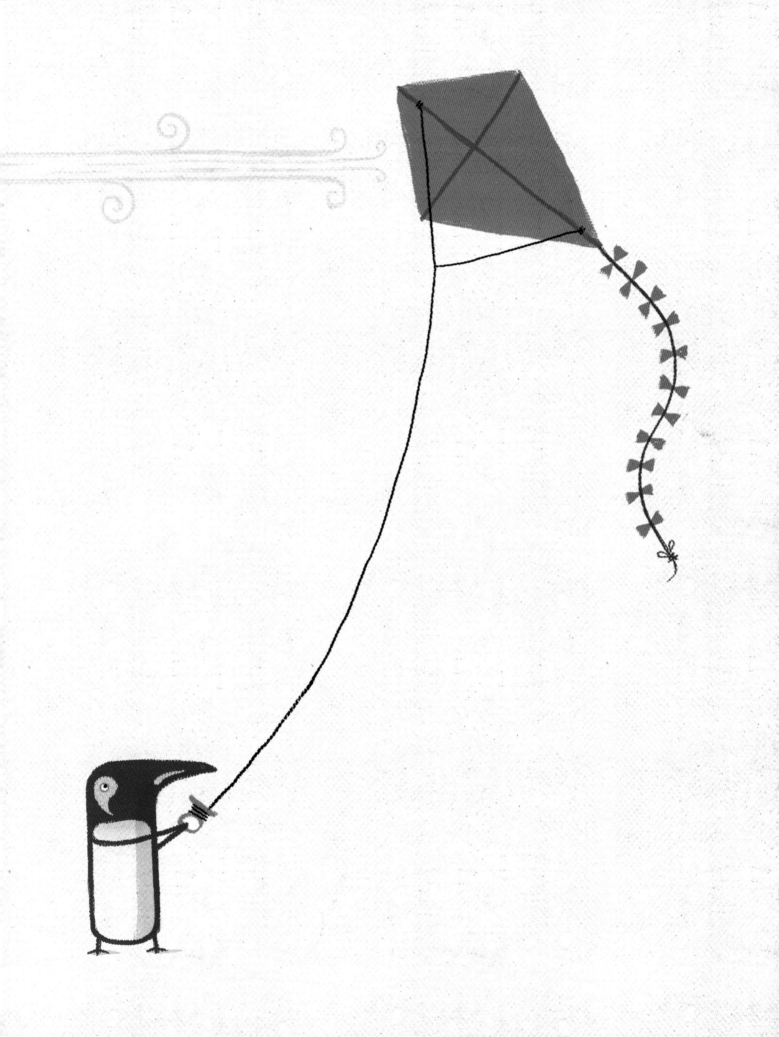

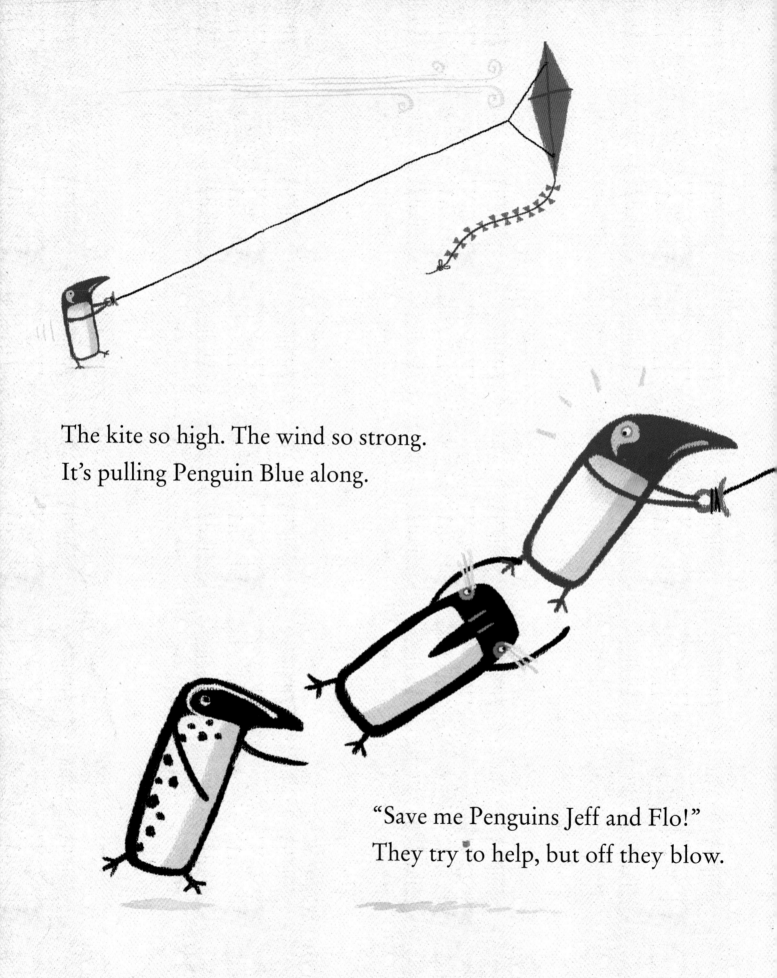

The kite so high. The wind so strong.
It's pulling Penguin Blue along.

"Save me Penguins Jeff and Flo!"
They try to help, but off they blow.

Up, up, away!
See how they fly.
A penguin train
up in the sky.

Don't worry,
Wilbur's seen
their plight...

Oh dear. It seems
he's joined the flight.

Blue spies a bear.
"Oh, help us, do."

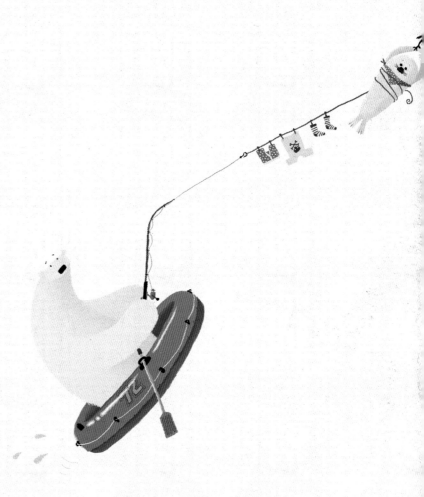

His name is Clive.
He's coming too!

Oh what a fix!
Oh my! Oh me!
The gang are flying
out to sea!

They swoop, they soar… in rain and shine…

They zoom straight through… clouds one to nine…

7 8 9

Past miles of
ocean far below.
Then… "LAND AHOY!"
shouts Penguin Flo.

A tiny island, lush and green
(A colour that they've never seen).
"The trees look soft, we'll be all right.
Hello jungle! Goodbye kite!"

"How nice," says Blue.
"A lovely spot.
Although it is
a bit too hot."

Jeff misses Mum.
Clive wants to go.

Oh dear. They can't. They're trapped. Oh no.

Intrepid travellers, never fear,   'Cos Blue has had a good idea.

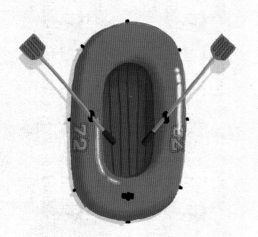

"The boat,

some leaves,

a vine and then...

...The wind will blow us home again."

One big gust
should get them going.
Now, who could help?
Who's good at blowing?

THE SEA
MORE SEA
EVEN MORE SEA
THE ANTARCTIC

THE SEA

MORE SEA

EVEN MORE SEA

THE A

They ride each crest and surf each wave,

Three cheers for five* companions brave.
*Is it five, or is it six? Somebody is playing tricks...

At last the chill of home – how nice
To feel your feet on solid ice.

A windy day.
Another kite.
"No thanks," says Blue,
"No trips tonight."

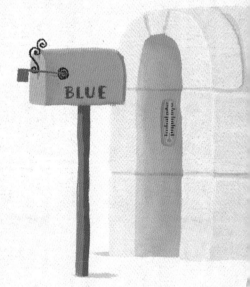

A lesson learned,
there's no denying,
This penguin wasn't
built for flying.